Maggie to the Rescue

by Ari Hill
illustrated by Judith Hunt

A GOLDEN BOOK • NEW YORK
Western Publishing Company, Inc., Racine, Wisconsin 53404

Mack and Maggie, two cats who were the
best of friends, lived in a furniture
warehouse. They had a wonderful life. They
slept long hours, chased mice, and shared
tidbits of food that Fred and Gus, the
warehouse workers, left for them.

The two cats often slept in the drawers of the furniture or on shelves. They loved the smell of new wood and the feel of the smooth-sanded boards.

One night Mack squeezed into the deep bottom drawer of a pine dresser. He snuggled way in the back and went to sleep. Maggie slept on a shelf.

The next morning, Maggie woke up and went to get a drink. While she was gone Fred and Gus came to load the pine dresser onto the delivery truck. Fred pushed the drawer shut, not knowing that Mack was inside. Away went the dresser! Away went Mack!

When Maggie came back, she stopped in the very spot where the dresser had been. "Mack," she called, "where are you?"

Scurrying back and forth, Maggie looked for the pine dresser. She couldn't find it. "What if it was taken away in the red truck that comes every day?" she thought. "That's where Mack must be—on the delivery truck!"

Frantically, Maggie jumped out a window
onto a catwalk overlooking the alleyway.
The delivery truck was nowhere to be seen.

Scampering down the ladder to the alley, Maggie knew she had to catch up with the truck before the dresser was unloaded. If she didn't, she might never see Mack again.

In the alley she met Henry. "*Psst*, Henry," she called. The large gray-and-white tomcat came shuffling out from behind a dumpster.

"Hi, Maggie. What's the matter?" asked Henry.

"It's Mack," Maggie answered. "He fell asleep inside a dresser that was taken away this morning in the big red truck. Did you see which way it went?"

Henry led Maggie to the street. "It went that way," he said, pointing with his paw.

"How will I know where to go from there?" asked Maggie.

"Just follow your nose," said Henry. "And good luck!"

"I must not think it's hopeless," Maggie told herself. "I must keep trying."

At the corner she met a tabby. "Did you see a big red truck pass by?" asked Maggie.

"Pass by!" said the tabby. "It nearly ran me over as it turned the corner."

"Thanks," said Maggie as she headed up
the side street. She ran along the block until
she came to a garbage can. She saw four
bushy tails peeking over the rim.

Maggie said, "Could you help me?" She
got no answer.

So Maggie sat down and started to cry. Finally the strangest-looking cat she had ever seen poked his head out of the can. "What's wrong?" he asked. Maggie quickly told him her story and asked if he had seen a big red truck go by.

"Oh, that truck," he said. "Yes, it went by, and it was leaking oil. Follow the oil."

Maggie saw the oil spots. She thanked the strange-looking cat and took off in that direction.

Maggie raced across town. At every house where the truck had stopped there was an oil puddle. And at every house Maggie prowled around and meowed until she was sure Mack wasn't there.

At last, too weary to go on, Maggie lay down on the grass in front of a white stucco house. She was even too tired to cry.

Inside the white stucco house a girl and
her mother had just opened the drawer
where Mack was trapped.

"Mother, look, a cat!" screamed the girl.

Mack gave a great big yawn and jumped
out of the drawer.

He quickly ran through the house and found an open window. He leapt through it, jumped over some bushes, and ran onto the front lawn.

Mack could hardly believe his eyes when he saw Maggie. Maggie could hardly believe her eyes when she saw Mack. They nuzzled each other and purred.

By evening Maggie had led Mack back to their warehouse. They were both weary and ready to go to bed. Mack jumped into an open cedar chest.

"I think it would be a good idea," said Maggie, "if you slept *on* the furniture instead of *in*! How will I ever find you if you get delivered again?"

So Mack curled up beside her on top of a
big maple desk, and they fell asleep
peacefully with the moon shining through
the window.